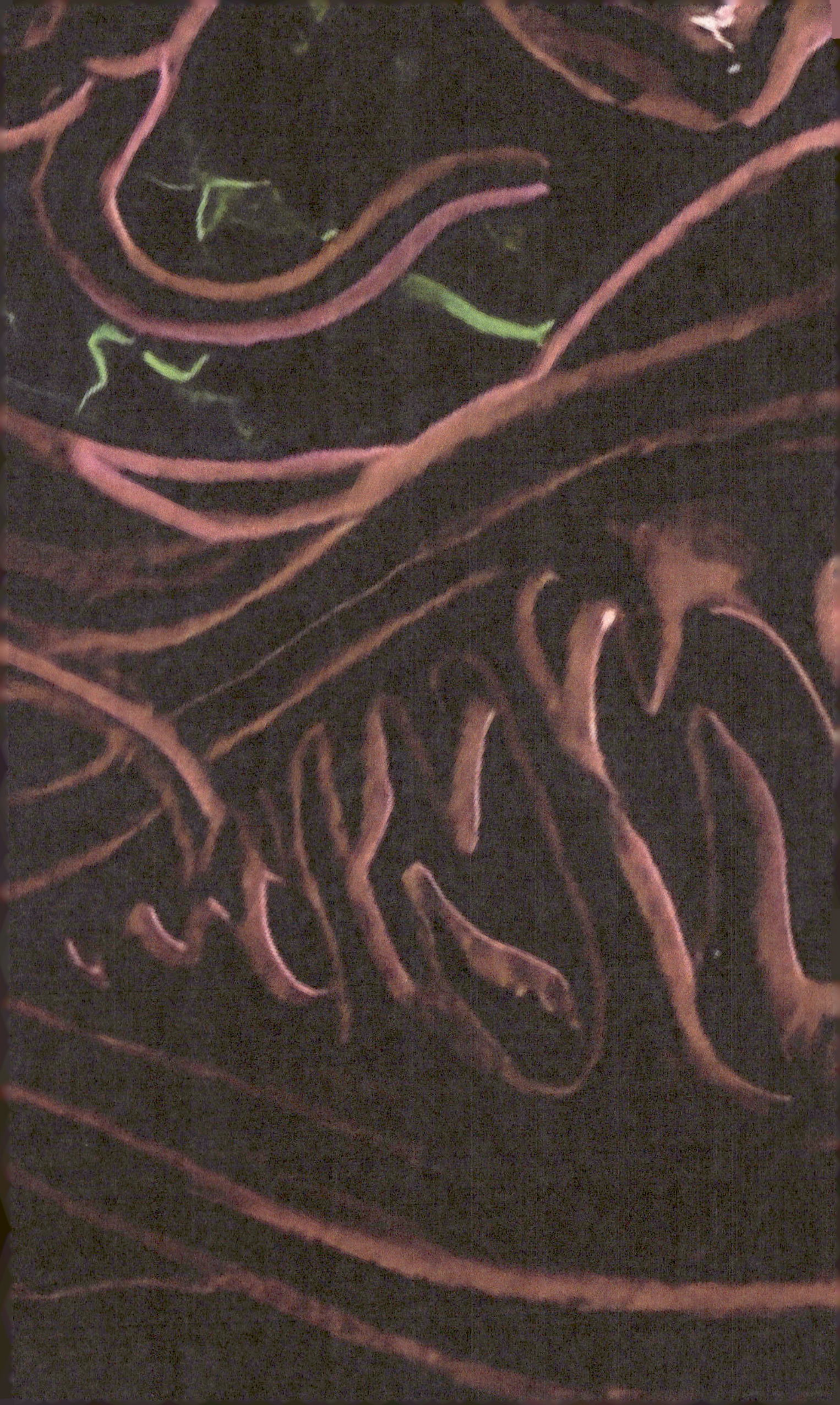

INHUMAN SKIN

BY MIKE DUBISCH

INHUMAN SKIN

BY MIKE DUBISCH

BOUND

Perhaps a vision sent you reeling
Mayhap a word unraveled all
A misstep, a slip, a trip, a stall
Many things can cause a fall

Maybe it was only they
Who could replace the locks
When it was you lost the keys
To the door of your house

A set of figures blown apart
Pieces of one soul
A formula of two parts
Combined to make one whole

What it is when one of two,
Dreaming they're awake
Every day is perfect,
Every day an Earthquake

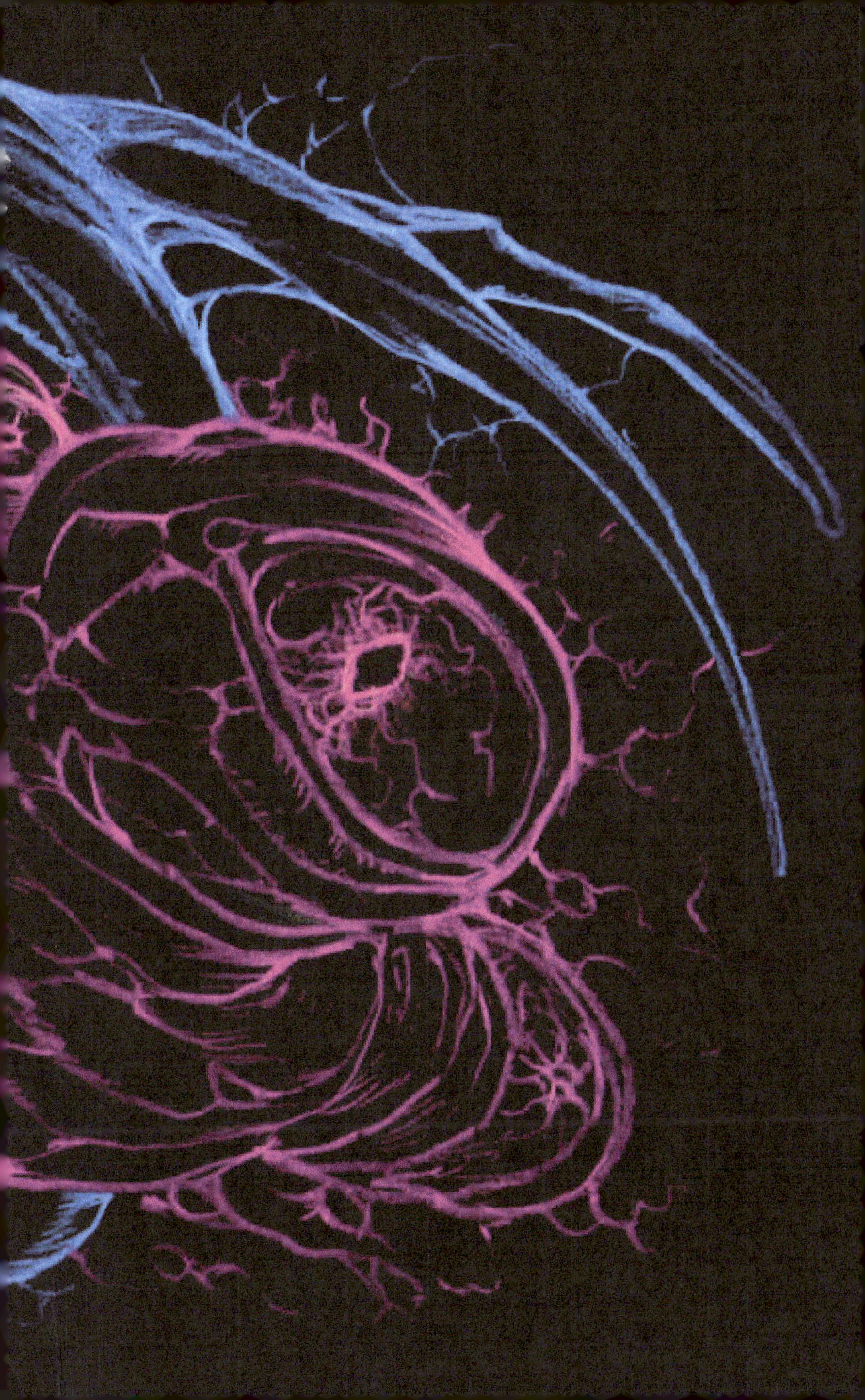

THE
DARK
LADY

She sneaks up behind you
She lurks up ahead
She hides all up inside you
She waits within your bed

She's staying with your loved ones
She's collared all your pets
She brought all of you your dinner
She's the reason you have sex

She's met with all your ancestors
She'll meet all your offspring too
She's lain with all within this world
She's without no doubt the blue

She is present when she isn't there,
And when she's there we're not,
She breathes our air,
She steals our share,
And parcels out the lot

Without her there could be no rot,
No rot, no mulch, no fruit
No fruit, no life, no meat, nor milk
No nectar, sap, or soup

She's the source of all your pain
Without her there's no gain
She makes everyone the same
You all know her by name
She'll treat you just the same

WORSHIP

Ten pearls lined up in rows of five
Two miles of curves
The cavern which births all lives
The two moons that serve

Lost in a shallow depression
The valley curve beneath
Two small watchtowers atop two hills
Two mountain ridges reach

Two thin branches end
With two tiny women
Each one also wears a pearl
On each of their five heads

Waterfall of silk, gazing pools of hue,
Breathing monument pointing to
Seashells hearing both false and true
Sweet red leaves a lick made new

ROOTS

Wings of wildfire, fall of wheat
Wave of darkest shade
Twin wells beckon with black blades
Two deadly strokes are made

Owning beloving our treasures our finds
The canyon upon which we lose our minds
Playing with the fire we desire to dowse
Entirely with our exclamation of self

Two gentle inclines support
Two hanging fruit comport
Four roots grow you'll see
From this great trunk of tree

The first two grasp at the world
Holding fast what they can entwine
A loyalty men cannot fathom
Truth impressed by tide and time

The second two roots wrap
'round their lover's back
And the sight is like sound blasting
Our armies, our legions, our children, our acts

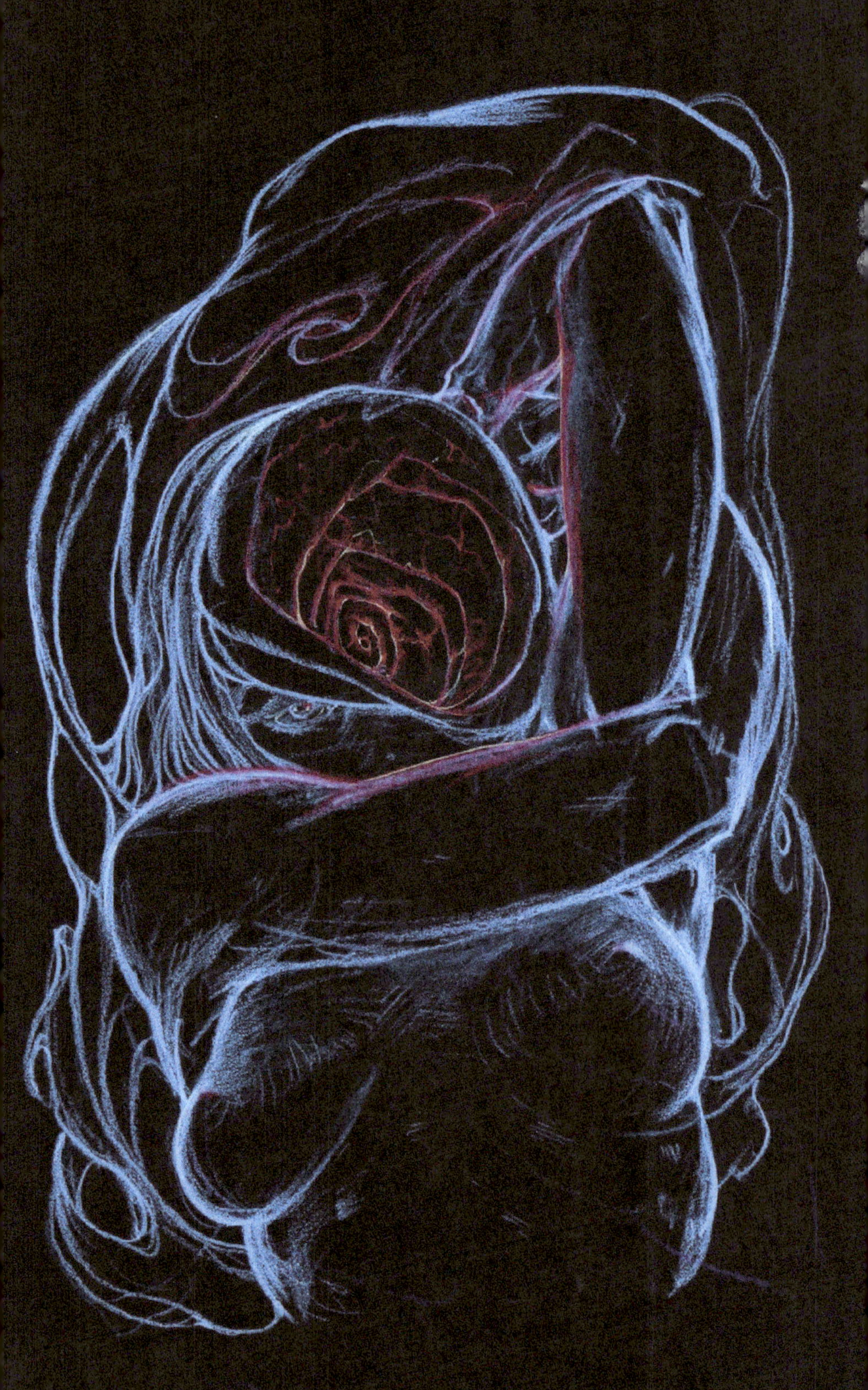

ENCHANTMENT

Sweet slice of pie or cake
Cherry tomato our souls ache
Navel not of an orange
Flower blooms where pleasure's found

Pale smooth candy coating
Two creampuffs draw the eye
Wall of color drives one mad
The cherries top our soul desire

Rich creamy candy rose
Tastes us as we taste them
Wine with effervescent nose
A reflection of us bleeds

Glossy clear pastilles entrance
A gaze that fills like sustenance
Above all these will enchant us
And bring us to our knees

MAGEFIRE

The perfect time of day
Framed by a fine halo of light
A stretch of land to bury yourself
A ledge from which to sight

Two visions that can be touched
A caged birds wing beats
Another halo to draw us into
The caverns that bring out the beast

The limbs among which we'd be enshrined
The palms into which we'd place our sign
The feet that carry this coveted prize
The musk that stokes the Magefire

CRAVES
THE
SEED

Craves the seed
We make for them
Raises the staff
We wear for them

Owns the absence
We'd fill for them
Wears the orbs
We scry for them

Moves the mountains
We scale for them
Works the spells
We'd cast for them

Bears the children
We place in them
Makes the milk
She pours for them

WRECKED

A mountain range of desire
A sacred tree line of trust
A journey of hills and valleys
An ocean with waves you must

Scale, climb, swim or trek.
Pursue until your ship is wrecked
Upon her shores, impulse unchecked
Solo member of her sect

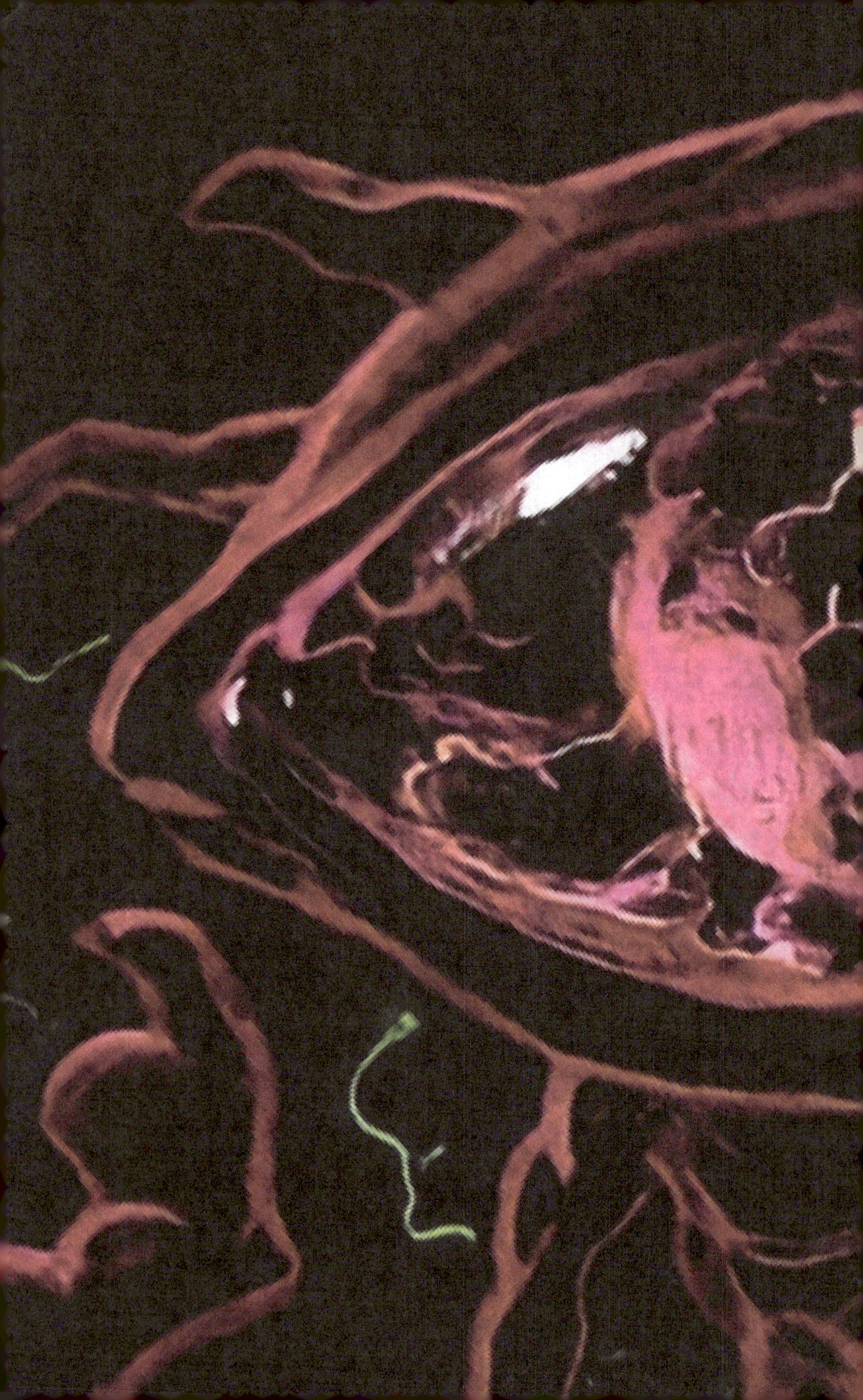

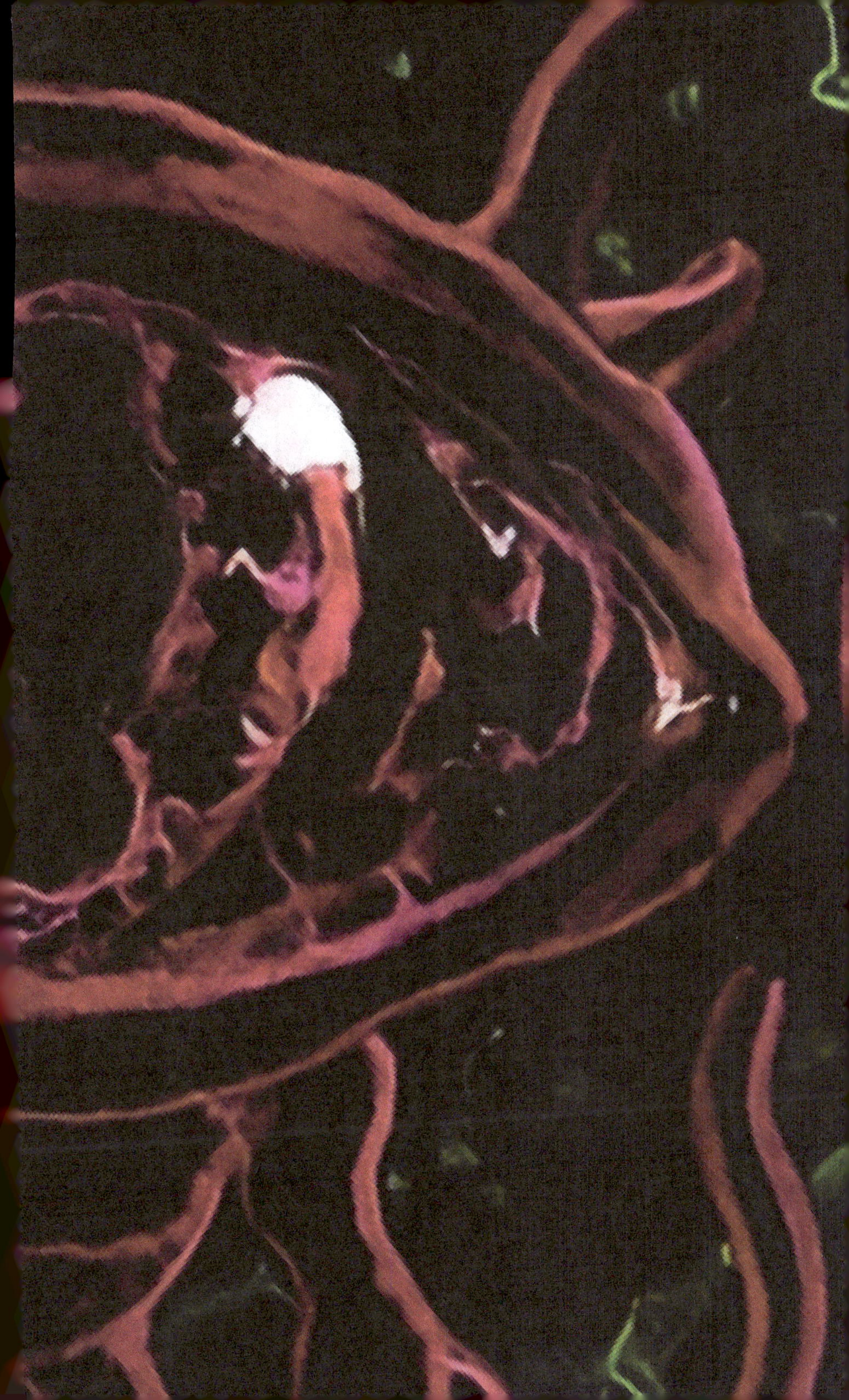

MIKE DUBISCH

This graphic novelist and illustrator has been creating and publishing comics and art since the 1980s. He has carved out a unique place creating horror, science-fiction, surrealism, and YA adventure works using all but lost traditional techniques. Born in California, USA, the artist has traveled and lived in five countries. He has been an instructor at the Academy Of Art University since 2012 and is married to children's book illustrator and sculptor Carolyn Watson Dubisch, with whom he has three daughters.

9 781960 213389